STAR WARS™

I AM A PADAWAN

By Ashley Eckstein

Illustrated by Shane Clester

A GOLDEN BOOK • NEW YORK

© & ™ 2020 LUCASFILM LTD. All rights reserved. Published in the United States by Golden Books, an imprint of Random House Children's Books, a division of Penguin Random House LLC, 1745 Broadway, New York, NY 10019, and in Canada by Penguin Random House Canada Limited, Toronto. Golden Books, A Golden Book, A Little Golden Book, the G colophon, and the distinctive gold spine are registered trademarks of Penguin Random House LLC.

rhcbooks.com

ISBN 978-0-7364-4046-2 (trade) — ISBN 978-0-7364-4047-9 (ebook)

Printed in the United States of America

10 9 8 7 6 5 4 3 2 1

I am a Padawan.

I am a young **Jedi in training**.
A Jedi protects the galaxy from harm.

In order to become a Jedi Knight, a Padawan must be strong with the **Force**—an energy field created by all living things.
The Force is strong with **Ahsoka Tano**.

When Ahsoka was little, a Jedi Master named Plo Koon sensed her **power** and brought her to the Jedi Temple for training.

Jedi Master **Yoda** helped train Ahsoka and other Force-sensitive children, called **younglings**, so they could become **Padawans**.

Yoda taught his students to use the Force for **knowledge and defense**—never for attack—and warned them to control emotions like anger and fear, which lead to the dark side of the Force.

When younglings become
Padawans, they are paired with a
Jedi Knight, who will continue
to teach them the ways of the Force.

Anakin Skywalker—
one of the most powerful Jedi of all
time—took Ahsoka as his Padawan.

The best way for a Padawan to learn is through experience. As Anakin's Padawan, Ahsoka was eager to prove herself in the **Clone Wars**, fighting alongside Anakin, Jedi Master Obi-Wan Kenobi, and a loyal clone trooper named Captain Rex.

A Padawan must learn to **make new friends** and work well with others.

Barriss Offee was also a Padawan, but she was very different from Ahsoka. Barriss did whatever her Jedi Master told her to do, while Ahsoka liked to **ask a lot of questions** before she agreed to do something.

Barriss and Ahsoka learned to look past their differences and became good friends.

A Padawan **learns** from their mistakes and listens to their teachers.
When Ahsoka did not listen to Anakin's orders, she failed at her mission.

It is also important for a Jedi Padawan to be selfless and **help others**, no matter what the cost.

When Senator Padmé Amidala was in danger, Ahsoka raced to help her right away!

Sometimes Padawans find themselves in scary situations, but they must be **brave** and rely on their Jedi training.

Ahsoka **defended** herself against enemies like **General Grievous**, **Asajj Ventress**, and **Cad Bane**.

A Padawan passes on the **lessons** they've learned to others.

Ahsoka trained rebels on Onderon to defend themselves from the droid army . . .

. . . and taught a group of younglings how to build their own lightsabers.

A **lightsaber** is the weapon of a Jedi Knight. Every lightsaber is different and special to its owner.

Ahsoka has **two** lightsabers!

In certain situations, a Padawan has to slow down and have **patience**.

When Ahsoka lost one of her lightsabers, she had to learn to quiet her mind and calm her worries in order to find it.

More than anything, Padawans must learn to
trust in themselves.

When Ahsoka was accused of something she
didn't do, she had to learn to stand up for
herself—even when it felt like no one but Anakin
believed her.

And a Padawan should always have **hope**, no matter how dark things seem.

Ahsoka never gave up when she was on trial for a crime she did not commit. She knew the Jedi Council would discover the **truth** that she was innocent, and they did!

Sometimes Padawans have to make **tough decisions**.

Ahsoka decided to walk away from the Jedi Order to follow **her own path**.

Every Padawan has a different journey.
Where will **your journey** take you?

Are **you** ready to become a **Padawan**?